Summary: A couple of chipmunks make new
friends and learn to trust.

For our precious miracle, Ariana, who blesses us with her brilliant and loving smile every day.

To you, Victoria, thank you for always being our champ. We love and cherish you both more than words could ever express.

For Olivia and Ethan, my sweet babies.
I love you more than you will ever know.
My heart is bigger because of you.
Love you always and forever.

Magical Lake

A Buddy & Swifty Chipmunk Champs Series Adventure

By A.C. Szul, with Victoria A. Szul

Illustrated by Rigina Pietrowski

"The sky is clear tonight — stars are bright and seem so close," said Swifty, looking up from highest point on the bungalow roof.

"Yeah, can't get a better view on a night like this," said Buddy, as he listened to the calming sound of crickets in the Pocono Mountains.

The two chipmunk best friends were relaxing after a fun-filled summer day.

Swifty fell asleep, near the bungalow's side gutter.

A short time later, Buddy drifted to sleep.

Swifty rolled to the roof's edge and slid gently down the gutter.

The chipmunk landed softly inside a boy's bicycle basket, on top of a baseball cap.

On the back of the bike's seat a hanging tin license plate read "Sam" in red, white and blue colors.

Swifty just kept snoring. When Sam got on his bike, he did not notice the furry little passenger.

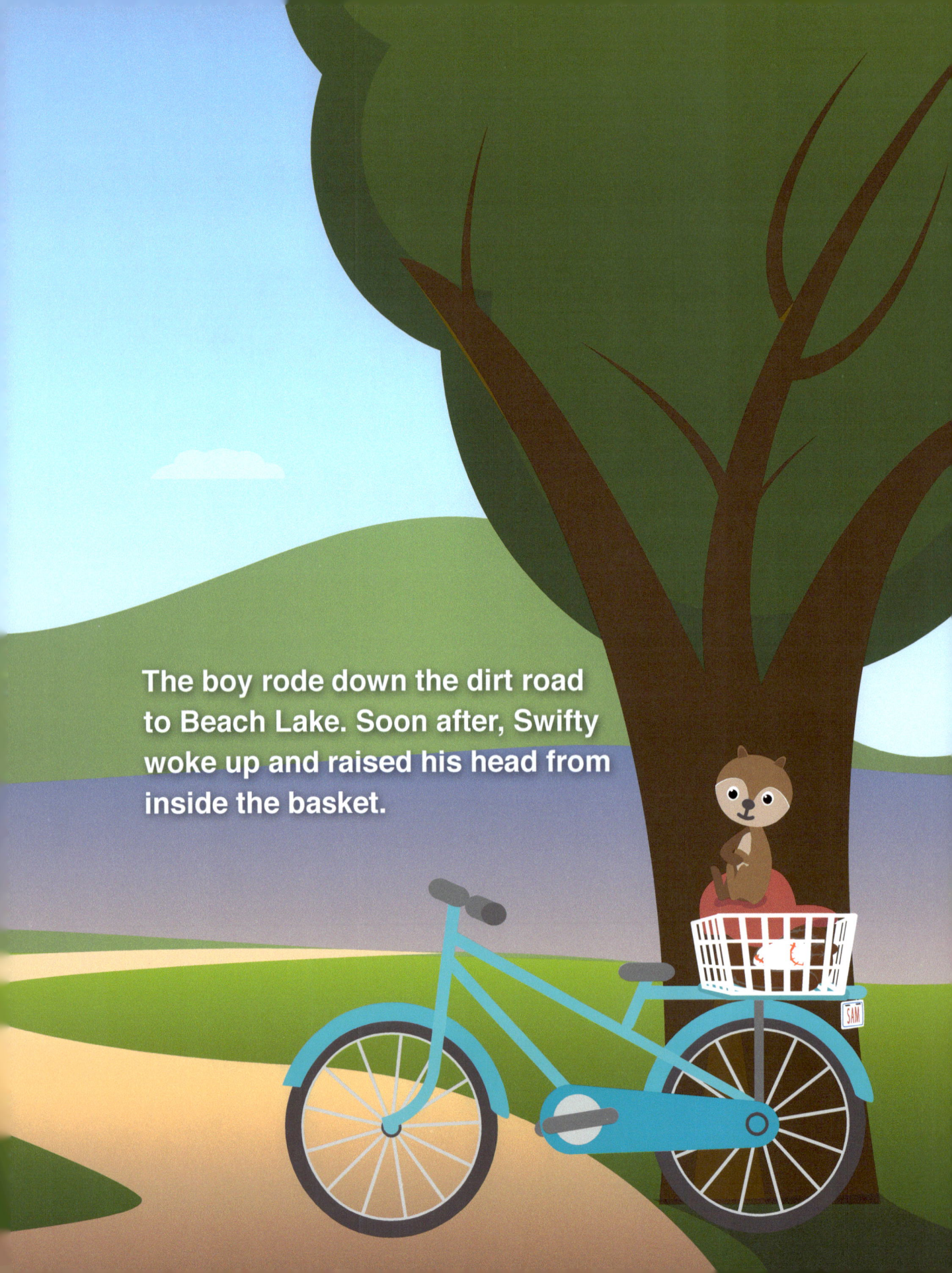

The boy rode down the dirt road to Beach Lake. Soon after, Swifty woke up and raised his head from inside the basket.

As Swifty climbed out and walked toward the lake, he saw a girl chipmunk standing proudly on a raft.

The raft, made of small branches, was floating close to the lake's sandy shore.

"Hi, there," called out Swifty, waving his hand. The girl chipmunk smiled, looking at Swifty.

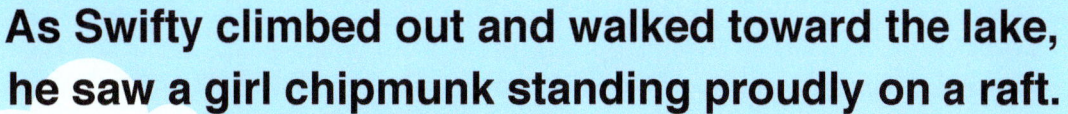

She looked friendly. "What's your name?" asked the girl chipmunk. She wore a large purple bow on her head. "I'm Swifty, from up the road, nearby the bungalows." "Nice to meet you, Swifty," she said.

"My name is Annie. Are you here to swim?" "Huh, well … I've actually never been in the water," he said. "Climb aboard, Swifty. We can explore the lake," said Annie. "It's a beautiful view from the center of the lake. Trust me."

"I don't know, I'm just not …" said Swifty.

"Oh, come on, making new friends is fun," she said. "You'll enjoy the ride on my raft." Annie placed a branch in the water and pushed.

Sitting on the raft, with his feet dangling just above the water, Swifty leaned back against one of the twigs. As they moved further out to the middle of the lake, everything on the shore appeared to get smaller.

Waves slapped gently against the sides of the raft.

Swifty watched as Annie dived into the water and popped back up to the surface.

"Do you come here often?" asked Swifty. "Yup, the lake is my most favorite place," she said. "Swimming is also super exercise."

The sun was bright and the water was warm.

"Hey, what's that – over there," said Swifty, pointing to what seemed like a tail poking out of the water. Suddenly a head appeared. It turned in the direction of the two chipmunks. It looked like a seahorse. And then it spoke. While the two chipmunks were surprised, they quickly realized the creature was friendly.

"Hi, I'm Zora," she said.

Both Swifty and Annie introduced themselves. Zora invited them to visit her home, far below the lake's surface. As the chipmunks followed Zora, they were magically able to breathe underwater.

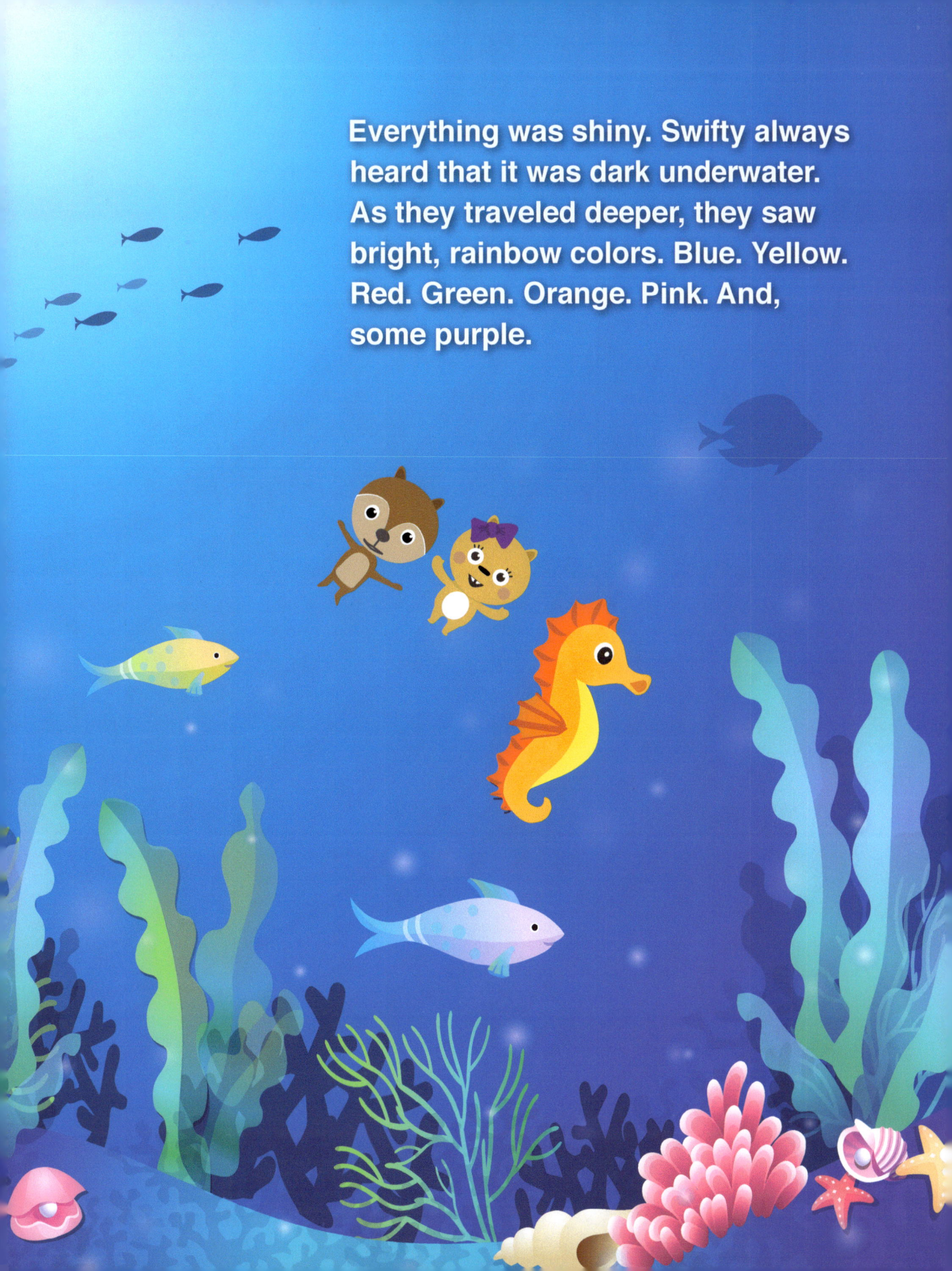

Everything was shiny. Swifty always heard that it was dark underwater. As they traveled deeper, they saw bright, rainbow colors. Blue. Yellow. Red. Green. Orange. Pink. And, some purple.

There were huge caverns along the lake's bottom, with sparkling bushy trees lining pathways. Could this be for real, wondered Swifty.

"Do you like what you see?" asked Zora, turning to Swifty.

"Wow," he said. "It's beautiful. Like nothing I've ever seen or even imagined."

The other seahorses were different sizes and colors.

Everyone appeared happy and welcoming toward the chipmunks.

"Zora, I had no idea how nice it was here," said Annie.

As Swifty started to move up to the lake's surface, a cold raindrop fell on his nose. When he opened his eyes, he looked across the field.

From the bungalow roof, he watched the sunrise. He was completely dry – except for a passing sprinkle.

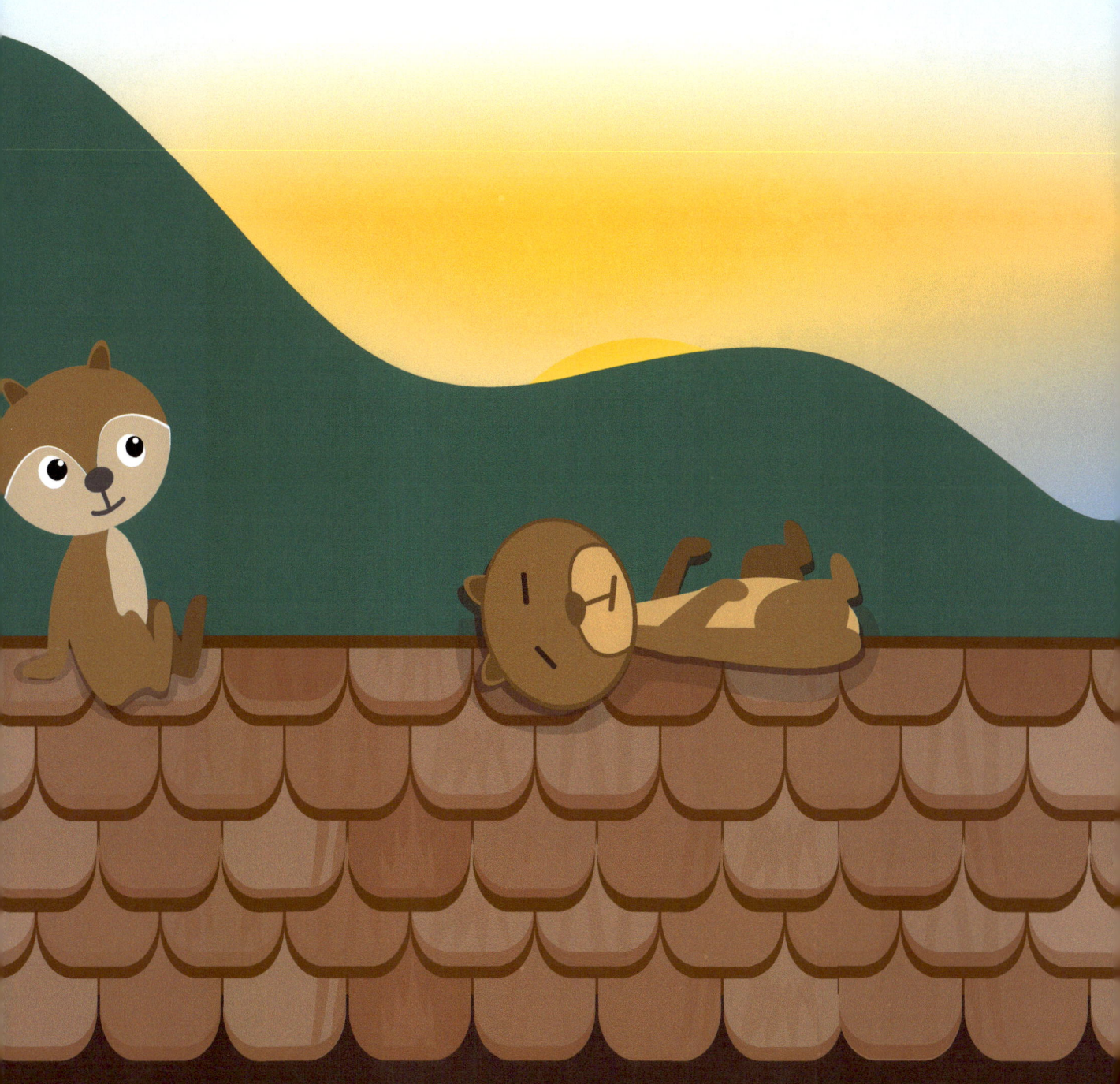

There was no bike, no side gutter, and he was far from Beach Lake. He felt stronger inside and more confident. The incredible adventure was a dream. But what he experienced and learned would stay with him forever.